I am dedicating this book to my grandson, Henry Wayne

Joy's Journey

Joy galloped through the field. **This is boring**, he thought.
Nothing's special around here.
"Hey, Roscoe," said Joy, "I'm not happy on the farm.
There's got to be more than just this."

Roscoe looked up from munching on some grass. "What do you mean? I love it here. We're well taken care of. We have food and shelter and lots of friends. What more can you want?"

With a snort, Joy shook his head. "I don't know. But I know this life isn't for me. There's something missing." "Ha," said Roscoe. "The last time you thought something was missing, you ran off and almost got eaten by coyotes."

"Awh, that was last year," said Joy. "The other day, Farmer Rangle had a magazine with a picture of rainbow unicorns with sparkles and jewels."

"That's what I want. I know having blingy stuff will make me happy."

"You don't know what's good for you." Roscoe swished his tail and went back to grazing.

Joy watched all the horses strolling around the field. This life is definitely not for me, he thought. I'm going to leave when everyone is asleep.

The discontented horse waited till it was dark.
When the time was right, he jetted out through
the field and leapt over the fence. He ran all night.

In the morning, Joy saw what he was looking for.
"It's the mall!"

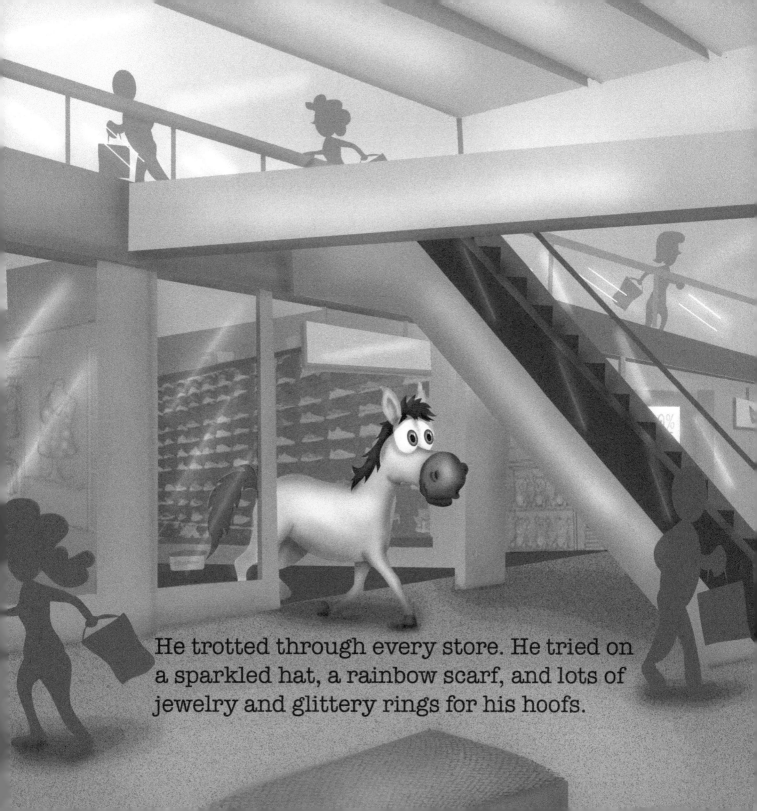

He trotted through every store. He tried on a sparkled hat, a rainbow scarf, and lots of jewelry and glittery rings for his hoofs.

As he looked in the mirror, he smiled. "Whoa! I look great. I'm one fancy, handsome horse. Everyone will be impressed when they see me."

He roamed the mall, but soon got bored. "I look flashy, but I need more." That's when he saw a sign for a concert. **I could use some excitement**, he thought. **I'll have fun and everyone can see my new look.**

Joy galloped to the concert. The place was jammed-packed with people laughing. Look at how happy they are, he thought. Soon, the guitars and drums blared. Joy swayed to the music.

He had lots of fun until the concert ended and the crowd left. Joy felt lonely. He felt more unhappy than he had been on the farm. "There's no one to see my fancy clothes and jewels," he whispered.

"I need something else."

Not sure what to do, Joy trotted along a road until he came to a mansion with the biggest barn he'd ever seen. "Now, that's what I need. If I could live in a barn that grand, I'd finally be content."

Trotting into the barn, he said, "Hi, I'm Joy."
The horses ignored him.
Hmm, he thought. **Back home everyone is so friendly and nice.**

Joy walked around the stalls. From the horseshoes to the barn doors, everything looked like it was made of gold. This is amazing, he thought. **Even the horses look fancy.**

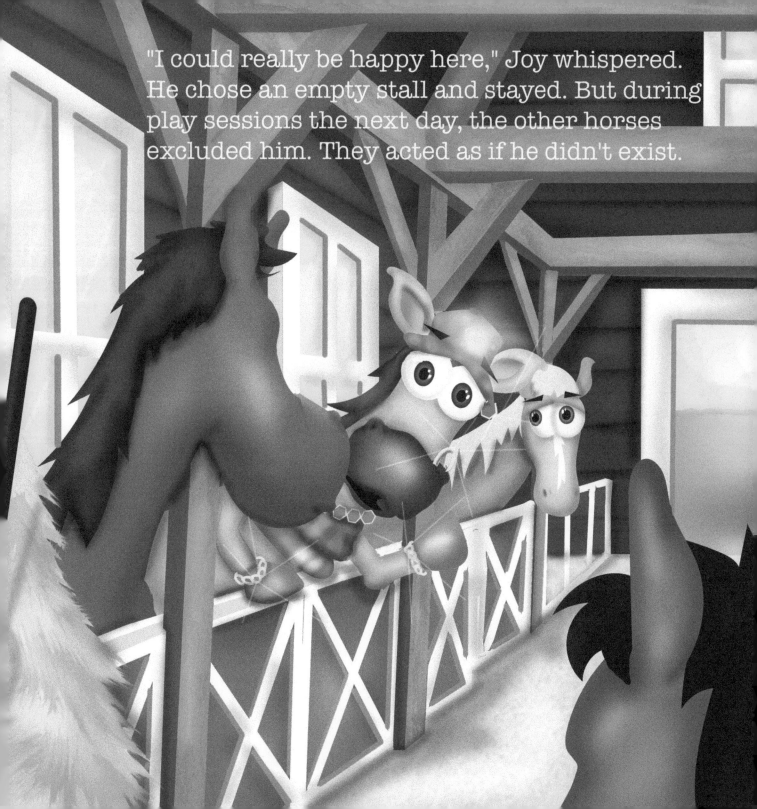

"I could really be happy here," Joy whispered. He chose an empty stall and stayed. But during play sessions the next day, the other horses excluded him. They acted as if he didn't exist.

Joy's heart sank. "I've never felt so alone and sad. This can't be the answer to contentment. I don't belong here." Joy trotted along until he came to a car dealership.

The cars were beautiful. They were so shiny his reflection sparkled in the sunlight. **Look at all those horses and people admiring the cars,** he thought.

"Having one of those fancy cars would make me happy and everyone would envy me," said Joy.

He bought the most expensive one. It was the reddest and shiniest of them all.

With the top down, the sun and wind felt wonderful. "This is happiness," shouted Joy. He drove all over the countryside until the sun began to set.

"B-Brrrrr," Joy stuttered as he put the top up. He sat in his fancy car shivering and sad ... and all alone. A tear welled up in his eye.

Why can't I be happy and content, he thought? What's wrong with me? I tried everything. There's got to be more.

The next day, Joy brought the car back to
the dealership and left all his fancy stuff in it.
Then he wandered down the road.

Joy thought of his friend Roscoe. We had a lot of fun. We laughed and played all the time. We shared our toys as young colts and played horse games until bedtime.

Just thinking about his friend and the farm made Joy smile, inside and out.

"Maybe I was wrong," he whispered. "Maybe it's not the flashy, expensive things that bring happiness."

Joy found himself trotting and then galloping back to the farm. "I finally know what happiness is," shouted Joy. "It's family and friends and being kind to one another. Wait till I tell Roscoe!"